Bear in Love

Daniel Pinkwater   illustrated by Will Hillenbrand

CANDLEWICK PRESS

A bear lived in the woods. He had a little cave, just big enough for him.

Every morning, the bear would crawl out of his cave,
rub his eyes, stretch, and feel the morning sun.
Then he would look around for something to eat.

This particular morning, the bear saw something on the flat rock in the clearing outside his cave.

"What is that?" the bear said. It was orange and long and pointy and had green bushy leaves at one end.

"It smells nice," the bear said. "It might be good to eat." He nibbled it.

"It is crunchy. It tastes good, too! Yum!"

He went off through the woods, singing a song
to himself:

"*Very good, very good*
Very good indeed
Very good, yum yum yum
Very good indeed."

The next morning, when the bear crawled out of his cave . . .

"Look! Two more of them! Two more of those crunchy things! Someone must have left them for me. I wonder who."

He went off through the woods, singing a song
to himself:

> *"I wonder who*
> *I wonder who*
> *I wonder who, hum, hum, hum*
> *I wonder who."*

The next morning, when the bear crawled out
of his cave . . .

"Crunchy things! Three of them!
I will eat two now and
save one for later."

But he ate them all.

"Someone is nice to leave these for me," the bear thought. He went off through the forest, singing a song to himself:

"*Someone is nice*
Someone is nice
Very good, yum yum yum
I wonder who."

The next morning . . . "What? What? What, what, what? A whole bunch of them? Someone must like me to leave these good things!"

He went off through the forest singing a song
to himself:

"*Someone must like me*
Someone is nice
Very good, yum yum yum
Someone is nice."

The bear followed some bees. He followed them to a hollow tree. In the hollow tree, there was a beehive.
"Honey!" the bear thought.

The bees were angry, but the bear didn't care.
He scooped out chunks of honeycomb with his
claws. He licked the honey and got all sticky with it.

"I will eat all this honey," the bear thought.
"No, not all. I will save some for . . . for . . .
the nice . . . for the nice friend!" He went
through the woods, singing:

> "*Sticky honey*
> *Nice nice*
> *Sticky honey*
> *Nice nice.*"

The bear left the honeycomb on the flat rock.
He watched from the mouth of his cave.
He wanted to see who came to the flat rock.
He wanted to see who had left him the nice things.
He wanted to see who came, and he wanted to
see the friend find the honeycomb.

But he fell asleep. When the bear awoke,
the sun was shining, the honeycomb was gone,
and there was a flower on the flat rock.

"This is frustrating," thought the bear while smelling the flower. "I wonder who it is."

All day he sang a song to himself:

"I wonder who it is
I wonder who it is
I wonder who it is."

That night, the bear left blueberries on the rock. He stayed right beside the rock and tried hard not to fall asleep—but he did.

In the morning, every blueberry was gone, and there was a cookie on the rock. It was a big cookie, and it had raisins.

"This is special," the bear thought as he ate the cookie. "This is extra special." And he sang:

> "Extra special
> Extra special
> Extra special
> Extra special."

The bear went down to the road,
where he usually did not go.

He lifted a chocolate bar with only two
bites missing out of a trash basket and
took it to the flat rock.

"Extra special," the bear thought. He hummed and thought about what it would be like for someone to find the chocolate bar.

"*Hum hum*
   Ha ha
   Hum hum
   Ha ha."

A few nights after leaving the chocolate bar with only two bites missing on the flat rock, the bear was sitting in the moonlight when he heard someone singing a beautiful song and thought he saw a shadow flit across the clearing.

The bear sang a song, and he had a feeling someone was listening.

The next night, as the bear sang a song, he saw
someone peeking out from the bushes.

"You are some cute little bear," the bear said.

"And you are quite the big strong bunny."

(You might think there would be some confusion
at this point, but apparently not.)

"Those things you first left," the bear said.

"Carrots," the bunny said. "They are much favored by bunnies."

"Imagine that," the bear said. "How did you like the chocolate bar?"

"I thought it was extra special."

"I hoped you would."

And the two of them sat side by side in the clearing, singing songs as the sun went down.

For Jill, who is sweet and crunchy
D. P.

For Ann, who is extra special
W. H.

Text copyright © 2012 by Daniel Pinkwater
Illustrations copyright © 2012 by Will Hillenbrand

First edition 2012

Library of Congress Cataloging-in-Publication Data is available.
Library of Congress Catalog Card Number 2011046620
ISBN 978-0-7636-4569-4

12 13 14 15 16 17 LEO 10 9 8 7 6 5 4 3 2 1

Printed in Heshan, Guangdong, China

This book was typeset in Aged.
The illustrations were done in mixed media.

Candlewick Press
99 Dover Street
Somerville, Massachusetts 02144

visit us at www.candlewick.com